IDWAL

A Tall Tree and some Tall Stories

This book belongs to:

Name...

WRITTEN BY CAROL BARRATT

ILLUSTRATED BY WENDY HOILE

Thoughts from Carol

A big THANK YOU to SALLY KNIGHT
&
LORNA and JOHNNY FRANCIS.
Without the help and encouragement of these three friends,
this book would never have been written.

A big THANK YOU to all the animals and birds
who regularly visit my old mill in South Wales.
Without THEM, this book would never have been written!

In an old stone mill-house, deep in the Welsh countryside, a little girl called Astrid May is staying with her grandparents. She loves to hear the stories that her grandmother tells her. Stories about animals, birds and trees.

This book is a collection of her favourite stories about Idwal, her favourite tree. She likes to hear these stories over and over again.

Idwal is an old crack willow tree. In the early evenings he tells all the animals nearby to gather at the bottom of his trunk. He then tells them stories. Some are true stories and some are 'Tall Stories'. Only Sir Oswald Owl is wise enough to know which are true and which are not.

Can you spot Sir Oswald Owl?

Astrid May asks: "Why is Idwal called a crack willow?"

Her **Grandmother** answers: "Because from time to time twigs, and even branches, snap off crack willow trees and fall to the ground."

Astrid May asks: "What is a tall story?"

Her **Grandmother** answers: "A story that is exaggerated, boastful or even untrue. Sometimes a story *sounds* like a tall story, when it is in fact a **true** story."

EARLY ONE EVENING

Idwal says: "The wood from *my* tree is used for making cricket bats". He is a very proud tree.

The trio of rabbits say: "OOOOh Idwal. That *must* be a tall story."

Sir Oswald Owl says:
"Actually it's *not* a tall story. It's a **true** story. Cricket bats **are** made from crack willow trees."

I would like to play cricket if the bat were small enough.

Idwal says to a passing badger, "The weather has been quite cold recently, hasn't it? I saw a fox putting on some foxgloves yesterday."

The badger says: "Are you sure Idwal? If a fox has special foxgloves, why doesn't a badger have special badgergloves?"

The trio of rabbits say: "OOOOh Idwal. That *must* be a tall story."

Sir Oswald Owl says:
"Actually, it *is* a tall story.
Foxgloves are flowers,
not gloves!"

EARLY ONE EVENING

Idwal says: "Have you heard about Kingsley Kingfisher? Yesterday he caught the biggest salmon you've ever seen."

A heron, who happens to be passing by, says, "Ridiculous!"

The trio of rabbits say: "OOOOOh Idwal. That *must* be a tall story".

Sir Oswald Owl says: "Actually, it *is* a tall story. You do exaggerate, Idwal! It was just a small stickleback fish! Kingsley caught it in this very pond."

All three rabbits look up as the heron flies overhead.

Herons always look dressed for weddings. They look as if they're wearing Morning Suits!

Idwal, who is now proudly wearing a birdfeeder says, "Did you know that when a nuthatch bird comes down a tree, he descends head first?"
A robin, who happens to be passing by, says, "How crazy is that!"

The trio of rabbits say: "OOOOh Idwal. That *must* be a tall story".
All three rabbits giggle at the same time.

Sir Oswald Owl says:
"Actually it's *not* a tall story.   It's
a **true** story.   The nuthatch **does**
come down a tree headfirst."

So do squirrels.

Idwal says: "Great news. 'Idwal's Pipe Orchestra' has been asked to play at 'The Last Night of The Proms.' "

The trio of rabbits say: "OOOOh Idwal. That *must* be a tall story."

Sir Oswald Owl says:

"Actually it *is* a tall story.

'Idwal's Pipe Orchestra' has been asked to play at

'The Last Night of The Toms'---- a hideous, howling,

hissing, screeching, growling, meowing concert of

tom cats to be held in the next field!"

Astrid May asks: "What is 'The Last Night of the

Proms'?"

Her **Grandmother** answers: "It's the last night

of a festival of special concerts performed at The

Royal Albert Hall in London. One day I'll take

you there."

Can you spot the greater spotted woodpecker pecking at Idwal's tree trunk? It looks as if he is wearing short red trousers!

Idwal says: "Did you know that a group of owls is called 'A Parliament of Owls'?"

The trio of rabbits say: "OOOOh Idwal. That *must* be a tall story."

Sir Oswald Owl says: "Actually it's *not* a tall story. It's a **true** story. Owls are very clever and important birds. We can even turn our heads almost right round. We can look completely over one shoulder. We miss nothing!"

How many owls can you see? Oh, I've just noticed the round bird-feeder!

Idwal says: "Yesterday, Jenny Swan flew inland from her nest on the sea. She landed on our pond. Milly Moorhen, who is always on her own, was *so* pleased to see her."

A badger, who happens to be passing by, says, "Jenny looks so beautiful at night when the moon lights up her white feathers."

The trio of rabbits say: "OOOOh Idwal. That *must* be a tall story."

Sir Oswald Owl says: "Actually it *is* a tall story. Swans are sometimes seen in the sea, but they never *nest* in the sea. They nest in rivers, ponds or streams. Jenny swam to us from 'Fairyhill', the beautiful hotel upstream. It only took her a few minutes and then she strolled on to our pond."

Fairyhill Hotel

Idwal says: "I saw Ted Toad moving out of his hole by the stream last night. He was really upset. Apparently he had heard the owners of the old mill saying, "Let's have toad in the hole for lunch tomorrow.""

The trio of rabbits say: "OOOOh Idwal. That *must* be a tall story."

Sir Oswald Owl says: "Actually it's *not* a tall story. It's **true.** The mill owners did have 'Toad-in-the-Hole' for lunch today. It's the name of a meal with sausages, not toads! The sausages are put inside holes made in batter!"

Idwal says: "When we held 'Idwal's Olympic Games' yesterday, Phil Pheasant ran in the 100 metres race. He won the Golden Acorn Trophy Cup."

The trio of rabbits say: "OOOOh Idwal. That *must* be a tall story."

Sir Oswald Owl says: "Actually it *is* a tall story. Phil *flew* the second half of the race. What a cheat! He was disqualified, of course."

Astrid May asks: "Why have I seen pheasants *run* away not *fly* away from danger?"
Her **Grandmother** answers: "They are so heavy that too much flying makes them tired, poor things!"

Idwal says: "I saw a scary sparrow hawk yesterday. He swooped down and caught a big buzzard in his sharp claws."

The trio of rabbits say: "OOOOh Idwal. That *must* be a tall story."

Sir Oswald Owl says: "Actually it *is* a tall story. You do exaggerate, Idwal! The sparrow hawk swooped down and caught a small chaffinch not a great big buzzard."

Millie Moorhen, who is always on her own, runs off. She just doesn't know *what* to think!

For those of you interested in such things, I am told that the sparrow hawk's sharp claws are called talons.

Idwal says: "Phil Pheasant doesn't take food from these birdfeeders. He waits for the smaller birds, like blue tits, to attack the seeds and nuts in the feeders. Then he picks up the bits of food that have fallen to the ground underneath."

The trio of rabbits say: "OOOOh Idwal. That *must* be a tall story."

Sir Oswald Owl says. "Actually it's *not* a tall story. It's a **true** story. Phil always waits for the smaller birds to do all the hard work. Lazy, lazy Phil!"

Sometimes I wait for those bits of food, too!

12

Idwal says: "There's a thief about! Jenny's swan food has been stolen. Wilberforce Weasel, the master spy, thinks he's on the scent. He found a stinking goosefoot by the side of the pond, just where the kind owners of the old mill usually leave Jenny's food."

The trio of rabbits say: "OOOOh Idwal. That *must* be a tall story."

Sir Oswald Owl says:
"Actually it *is* a tall story.
A 'stinking goosefoot' is the
name of a plant that smells
of rotting fish! The real
thief has been caught."

The thief was
Phil Pheasant.

Idwal says: "See the green frog at the side of the pond? He started life in the pond as a black dot in a blob of jelly. Then the black dot became a wriggling thing, still in the pond, called a tadpole. The tadpole eventually turned into a frog. Amazing!"

The trio of rabbits say: "OOOOh Idwal. That *must* be a tall story. You must have made that up."

Sir Oswald Owl says: "Actually it's *not* a tall story. It's **true**. Truly amazing!! Tadpoles *do* turn into frogs!"

EARLY ONE EVENING

Idwal says: "Look at those three ducks on the pond. Look they're not moving. They aren't real. They are called 'decoy ducks'.

Yesterday a pair of real mallard ducks joined them on the pond. They swam close to the decoy ducks. They couldn't understand why they were so still. They even tried to 'quack' to them. The mallards were so confused that they flew away!"

The trio of rabbits say: "OOOOh Idwal. That *must* be a tall story."

Sir Oswald Owl says: "Actually it's *not* a tall story. It's a **true** story. The mill owners would love to have lots of real ducks on the pond. That's why they put those artificial 'decoy ducks' there. It's a pity that the real ducks didn't stay for long."

Astrid May asks "Yes, but what do the decoy ducks actually *do*?" Her **Grandmother** answers: "They are supposed to attract **real** ducks to the pond."

Idwal says to a passing buzzard, "Early this morning I saw three black crows crashing into the windows at the old mill. They were 'dive-bombing' the windows. They *must* have woken up the owners."

The trio of rabbits stop giggling. They say: "We heard them too. We are **really** angry but what can we do?"

The buzzard says: "Annoying birds, crows, and spiteful too. They are nothing but trouble.
We should make a scarecrow for the mill owners. Hopefully, that will scare the crows away."

Sir Oswald Owl says: "Actually that's a good idea, even though *I* didn't think of it. Let's all get busy."

I knew these branches would come in useful.

Idwal says: "Look what we have all helped to make. We love living here and the owners of the mill never bother **us**. Now we can make sure the crows never bother **them**.

Let's hope it works!"

Astrid May asks, "Will it work?"
Her **Grandmother** answers, with a sigh,
"Mmm, fingers crossed!"
Her **Grandfather** exclaims, "Flipping crows!"

What a scary scarecrow!

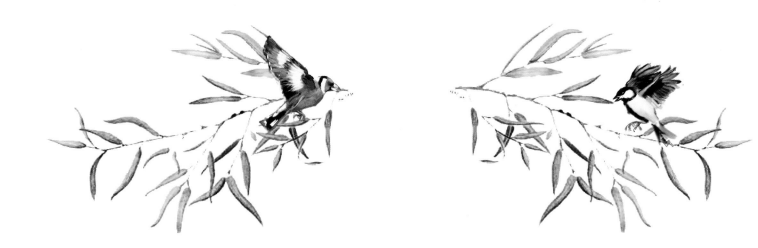

GOODBYE

Goodbye for now from Idwal. If you're in bed, goodnight and sleep tight.

Close your eyes and think of Idwal and his friends. (Sir Oswald, Phil, Kingsley, Jenny, Ted, Milly, Wilberforce, the trio of rabbits......

And the badger, the heron, the nuthatch, the robin, the woodpecker, the frog, the ducks......

OOOps, I almost forgot sweet little Meggie).

Zzzzzzzzzzzzzzzzz

I know Astrid May likes hearing about
Idwal at bedtime.
She'll be reading this book by herself
one day.
I know she'll soon be asleep.
Zzzzzzzzzzzzzzzzzzz

Published in 2017 by Peniarth.

University of Wales Trinity Saint David asserts its moral right
under the Copyright, Designs and Patents Act, 1988 to be identified
respectively as author and illustrator of this work.